BUMBLEBEE'S BIG MISSION

adapted by Patty Michaels

Ready-to-Read

Simon Spotlight

New York   London   Toronto   Sydney   New Delhi

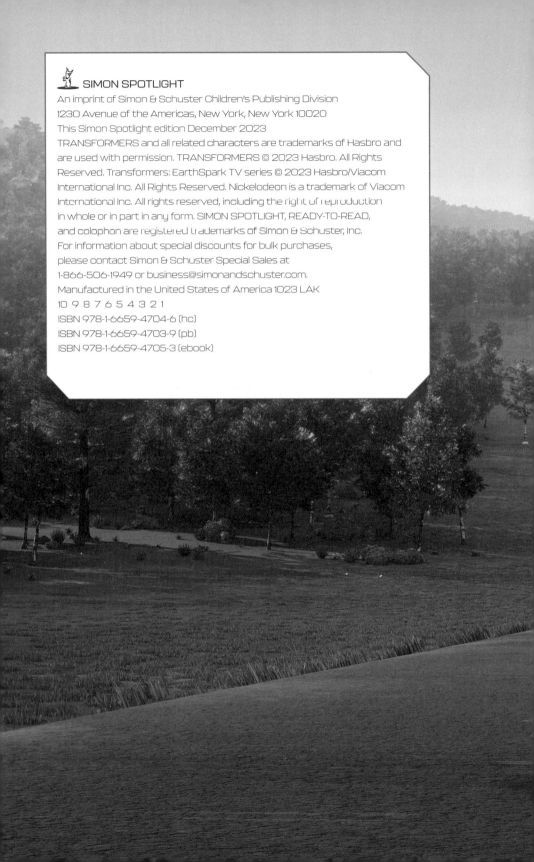

SIMON SPOTLIGHT

An imprint of Simon & Schuster Children's Publishing Division
1230 Avenue of the Americas, New York, New York 10020
This Simon Spotlight edition December 2023

For information about special discounts for bulk purchases,
please contact Simon & Schuster Special Sales at
1-866-506-1949 or business@simonandschuster.com.
Manufactured in the United States of America 1023 LAK
10 9 8 7 6 5 4 3 2 1
ISBN 978-1-6659-4704-6 (hc)
ISBN 978-1-6659-4703-9 (pb)
ISBN 978-1-6659-4705-3 (ebook)

Meet Bumblebee!

Bumblebee is a Transformers robot. He was born on a faraway planet, but now he lives on Earth.

He has a supercool alt mode.
He can convert into a yellow sports car
with black racing stripes!

Bumblebee loves to go fast
in his sports car alt mode!

Bumblebee is an Autobot.
Autobots are Transformers robots
who always do the right thing.

Optimus Prime, the Autobot leader,
trusts Bumblebee.

Bumblebee is a hero!
He lends a helping hand
to anyone in need.

For many years Bumblebee bravely fought alongside Optimus Prime and the other Autobots in the Transformers War.

When the war ended, Optimus Prime
started to work with people
to create a new world safe for humans
and Transformers bots.
But he needed a scout who could move
in secret without being traced.

Bumblebee was the perfect Autobot
for the job.

Then one day Optimus Prime learned that Transformers bots had been born on Earth.

These new bots, called Terrans, needed someone to teach them. Optimus Prime knew exactly who to call—his old friend Bumblebee!

The Terrans are part of the Malto family which also includes Dot, their mom; Alex, their dad; Robby, their brother; and Mo, their sister.

The Maltos live on a big farm in Witwicky, Pennsylvania.
Optimus Prime asked Bumblebee to live with the Maltos
and train the young Terrans.

At first Bumblebee didn't like his new assignment.

He had to sleep in a barn
with Twitch and Thrash.
The barn smelled like horses.
"Best mission ever," Bumblebee said
with a sigh.

Alex Malto was thrilled that
Bumblebee had come to live with them.
"Best mission ever!" he cheered.

Bumblebee had an important checklist
of things to do.
Most of all, he wanted to train
Twitch and Thrash as quickly as possible
so he could get back
to more exciting missions.

Dot Malto offered to make Bumblebee more comfortable in the barn. "If you want to add walls or anything else, be our guest," she told him.

"I appreciate that," Bumblebee replied.
"But training new recruits is a
pretty standard in-and-out mission.
I'll be gone before you know it!"

It turns out the Terrans were
not so easy to train.
They were having too much fun
exploring the human world.
They especially loved the
cute baby animals that lived
on the farm.

Mo and Robby Malto were happy
that Twitch and Thrash enjoyed being
part of their family.
They were having fun too!

But Bumblebee wasn't there to have fun.
He had a job to do.
"Let's go, Terrans!" he said.
"It's time to train!"

"I'm here on a serious mission," Bumblebee continued. "Optimus Prime tasked me with teaching a new generation. School is in session."

Bumblebee taught Twitch and Thrash important lessons,
like how to control when they changed into their alt modes.

He gave Twitch and Thrash important advice like, "A good scout considers every possibility before acting."

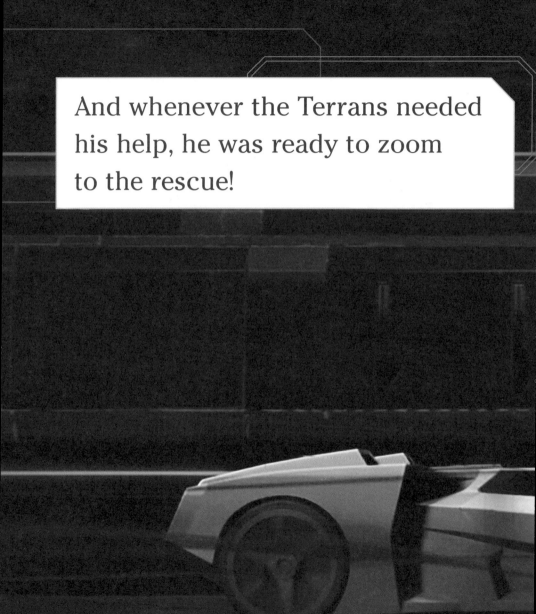

And whenever the Terrans needed his help, he was ready to zoom to the rescue!

It wasn't long after Bumblebee started to train them that the Terrans had learned enough to help him, too.

Soon Bumblebee noticed that he was not only training Twitch and Thrash, but he was having fun, too!
He loved game night, and he especially loved being part of the Malto family!

Bumblebee has been on many missions,
but this one is by far
his most important one ever.
He will never let his family down!